DETROIT PUBLIC LIBRARY

P9-EFJ-343

CHASE BRANCH LIBRARY
17731 W. SEVEN MILE RD.
DETROIT, MI 48235

FEB - 2004

For Suleiman, José, Naima,
Dagma, Flavia, Brunilda, Hagar, Jo, Hasna
and all the others who had to leave their first homes
and were brave enough to find new ones

—M. H.

For Christina

—K. L.

First published in the United States
by Phyllis Fogelman Books
An imprint of Penguin Putnam Books for Young Readers
345 Hudson Street, New York, New York 10014
Published in Great Britain
by Frances Lincoln Limited
Text copyright © 2002 by Mary Hoffman
Pictures copyright © 2002 by Karin Littlewood
All rights reserved
Printed in Singapore
1 3 5 7 9 10 8 6 4 2

Library of Congress Cataloging-in-Publication Data
Hoffman, Mary, date.
The color of home / Mary Hoffman ;
pictures by Karin Littlewood.
p.   cm.
Summary: Hassan, newly arrived in the United States and feeling
homesick, paints a picture at school that shows his old home
in Somalia as well as the reason his family had to leave.
ISBN 0-8037-2841-7
1. Somali Americans—Juvenile fiction. [1. Somali Americans—Fiction.
2. Refugees—Fiction. 3. Immigrants—Fiction. 4. Immigration and
emigration—Fiction. 5. Homesickness—Fiction. 6. Painting—Fiction.
7. Somalia—Fiction.] I. Littlewood, Karin, ill. II. Title.
PZ7.H67562 Co 2002
[E]—dc21   2001007393

The illustrations for this book were done in watercolor.

The Color of Home

MARY HOFFMAN

pictures by KARIN LITTLEWOOD

CHASE BRANCH LIBRARY
17731 W. SEVEN MILE RD.
DETROIT, MI 48235

Phyllis Fogelman Books New York

"We have a new boy joining us in school today,"
said Miss Kelly. "His name is Hassan and he's
from Somalia. I want you to make him feel at
home."

But the classroom didn't feel like home to
Hassan at all. In his real home he had lessons
outside from early in the morning until the sun
got too hot at midday. Here he had to stay
indoors except at recess, when he shivered
outside on the damp playground.

The children were friendly. They smiled at Hassan, and one of the boys kicked a soccer ball toward him. But he didn't understand anything that anyone said— only his name and "hello" and "bathroom." It was tiring remembering even a few English words.

After lunch, which Hassan didn't eat because he didn't know what it was, Miss Kelly gave all the children big sheets of paper and pinned them to easels. She gave Hassan paintbrushes and a jar of water, and showed him where all the colors were. He understood from her smiles and movements that she wanted him to paint a picture, but he had never done such a thing before.

He watched the other children for a while, then chose a bottle of bright blue.

He painted a blue, blue sky, without any clouds. Then a white
house, a yellow sun and mimosa trees. Outside the house
he made stick figures—himself, his father, his mother holding
a bundle that was his baby sister, his grandparents, his uncle,
his two cousins. There were nine people outside the house,
who all lived inside it.

Then Hassan took more paint and put in the animals—
a flock of white sheep, some brown goats, and a small sandy
creature that was supposed to be his cat.

"What a lovely picture, Hassan," said Miss Kelly.
"What beautiful bright colors!"

But Hassan hadn't finished. Now he chose red and orange and painted big flames on the roof of the house. The blue sky changed to a murky purple. He drew another stick figure, with a gun with black bullets coming out of it. He took the red paint again and splattered it on the white walls of the house. He smudged his uncle out of the picture.

"Oh, Hassan," said Miss Kelly. "It's all spoiled. What a shame!" Hassan didn't know what her words meant, but he heard the sadness in her voice and knew that she understood his picture.

"What did you do at school today?" asked his mother when she and his little sister, Naima, picked him up.

"Painting," said Hassan.

"Can I see?" she said. All around them, other children were showing their pictures to their parents.

"No," said Hassan. "The paint is still wet." He didn't want his mother to be sad. "You can see it tomorrow."

The next day Hassan wanted to tell Miss Kelly that he must make a new picture. But she had someone with her, a Somali lady wearing a black *hajab* like his mother's— only she also wore blue jeans and a black leather jacket, like a Western woman.

"Hello, Hassan," said the woman. Then she began to speak to him in Somali. "I'm Fela, I've come to translate for you and help with your English. Miss Kelly thought you might want to tell us about your picture."

So another teacher taught the rest of the class math, while Hassan sat in the reading corner with Fela and Miss Kelly and his picture.

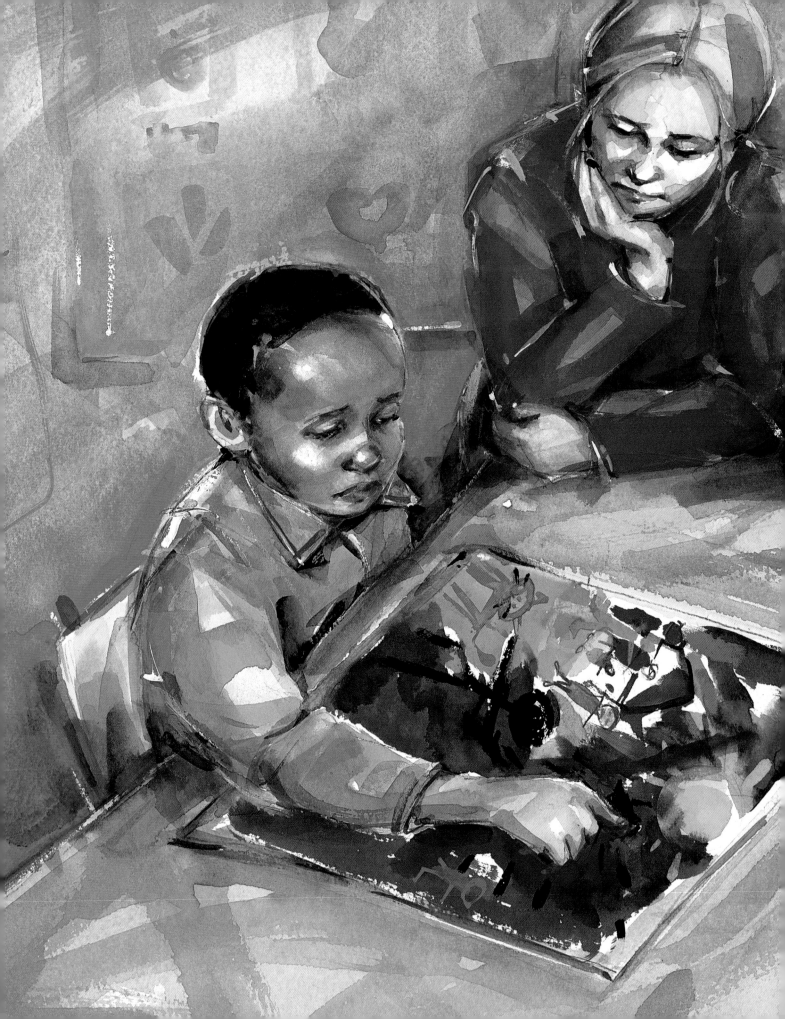

"That's my house in Somalia," he said, looking at Fela, who put his words into English. "That's my family." And he named them all, right down to the baby. "And that's my cat, Musa, who we had to leave behind."

"And who is this?" asked Miss Kelly, pointing to the smudge near the red splashes.

"That's my uncle Ahmed," said Hassan. And then he told them the whole story—about the noise, the flames, the bullets, and the awful smell of burning and blood.

"When the soldiers came, I hid in my cousins'
room," he said. "I didn't find out what happened
to my uncle until later. My father came and got me out from under
the bed and said we were leaving.

"We all left right away, except my uncle. We had no luggage, only my father's prayer mat and *qu'ran*, hidden in Naima's bag of diapers. I wanted to take Musa, my cat, but my mother said we must save ourselves and not the animals. I cried then, not for my uncle, but for Musa.

"We went on a big ship from Mogadishu to Mombasa. Then we lived in a camp for a long time. Naima learned to walk there. It was cold at night and my mother had to wait in line for all our food. People stole things, and all my mother's gold jewelry disappeared, but I think that was because we bought tickets to America. My cousins and grandparents stayed behind.

"I was frightened when I saw the plane we were going to fly in, because I thought it might have bombs in it. The journey was so long, but I wasn't happy when it was over. Our new country seemed all cold and gray. And the apartment we live in is gray too, with brown furniture. We seem to have left all the colors behind in Somalia."

Hassan talked for an hour and then he ran out of words, even in Somali. When he finished, Miss Kelly had tears in her eyes.

"Tell her I want to make another picture," Hassan said to Fela, "for my mother."

Then he played soccer with the friendly boy, who pointed to himself and said, "Jake."

That afternoon Hassan painted a new picture. It had blue sky, the white house, and the yellow sun. But this time there were no people—just sheep and goats and Musa the cat with his long spindly legs. There were no flames or bullets. By the end of the school day the picture was dry.

"It's beautiful," said
Hassan's mother.
"It's our home in Somalia,"
said Hassan.
"I know," said his mother.
"We'll put it on the wall of
our home here in America."
"Let me push Naima,"
said Hassan, and he walked
home pushing his little sister
in her stroller.

At home, they showed the picture to his father,
who stuck it on the wall. The blue, yellow, and white
looked bright against the gray paint. Next to it hung
the maroon prayer mat that had come with them on
their travels.

And as Hassan looked around the room, he saw other
colors—things his mother had made—a green cushion, an
orange tablecloth, and a pink dress she was sewing for Naima.

Just then the sun came out, and there was blue sky outside
their window. Hassan looked at his family and said, "Daddy,
can we have a new cat?" and he said "cat" in English. It was one
of the new words he had learned today.

Tomorrow he would ask Miss Kelly to tell him the word for "home."